The Hot Sun

by Mickey Daronco

I like the hot sun.
I can do a lot
in the sun.

It is fun to dig in the hot sun.
I fill my red tub.

It is fun to get wet
in the hot sun.
I go in for a dip.

I can be on a mat in the hot sun.
I rub it in. I do not want to get red.

I can get fit
in the hot sun.
I can hit with my bat.

Then I run and run.

I can sit
in the hot sun.
I like the sun a lot!